8/19

To: JADA & Zola

Aloha and Enjoy this
Reading Adventure!
Love
Papa & Nana

A Special Dedication

This book is dedicated to my best friend, Aaron Christopher Parker. Aaron and I became best friends in junior high. We remained best friends through high school, college, and into our adult careers. His life came to a sudden end on December 18, 2000 after he suffered severe head injuries in a car accident on an interstate highway. This book, written as a memorial for Aaron, illustrates a friendship between two Hawaiian animals and directly parallels my friendship with Aaron (Koa). This book is my "Thank You" to him — for you never get the opportunity to tell someone all of the wonderful things, both big and small, that he/she has done for you. After reading this book, please take a moment to — write a letter, make a phone call, send a text message, or even make a personal visit — to a special friend you need to thank.

ISLAND HERITAGE™
PUBLISHING
A DIVISION OF THE MADDEN CORPORATION

94-411 Kō'aki Street
Waipahu, Hawai'i 96797-2806
Orders: (800) 468-2800
Information: (808) 564-8800
Fax: (808) 564-8877
welcometotheislands.com

ISBN: 1-61710-283-0
First Edition, Fourth Printing—2018
COP 181707

The Kukui Tree

Written by Jarrod Gatlin
Illustrated by Don Robinson

ISLAND HERITAGE™
PUBLISHING

On the island of Kaua'i,
Where the water meets the land,
A wet and shiny monk seal
Was resting on the sand.

He settled himself on the perfect spot
Prepared to take a nap,
But just before he fell asleep
He felt a lightweight tap.

An 'ō'ō bird was at his side.
"Do you want to play?
Wouldn't you rather have some fun
Than waste away the day?"

"By the way," the 'ō'ō said,
"My friends all call me Koa.
My home is in the swamp up north.
Maybe someday I'll show ya!"

"My name is Hilo," said the seal.
"This is my home — Shipwreck Beach,
And sometimes I'm out at sea
Where only eyes can reach.

They took off to the northwest coast
And were taken by surprise
When Koa spotted something.
He could not believe his eyes!

Just above the canopy,
Where the treetops touched the sky,
A heavy rope was stretched way out
To the forest's other side.

Koa fluttered higher
To get a look around,
Then started doing somersaults
And jumping up and down!

6

He'd been waiting for a lifetime
To ride a zipline over land.
He turned to Hilo with a smile
And took him by the hand.

"Oh no!" said Hilo fearfully.
"You're not getting me on that!"
He backed himself a few short steps
And on the ground he sat.

"Hilo," begged Koa
"Can't you at least give it a try?
You never know, you just might like
Zipping through the sky!"

"A little courage is all you need
When trying something new.
Close your eyes, think happy thoughts,
That's all you have to do!"

And soon the quiet sky
Was filled with happy laughter,
As Koa came zipping by
And Hilo came right after!

8

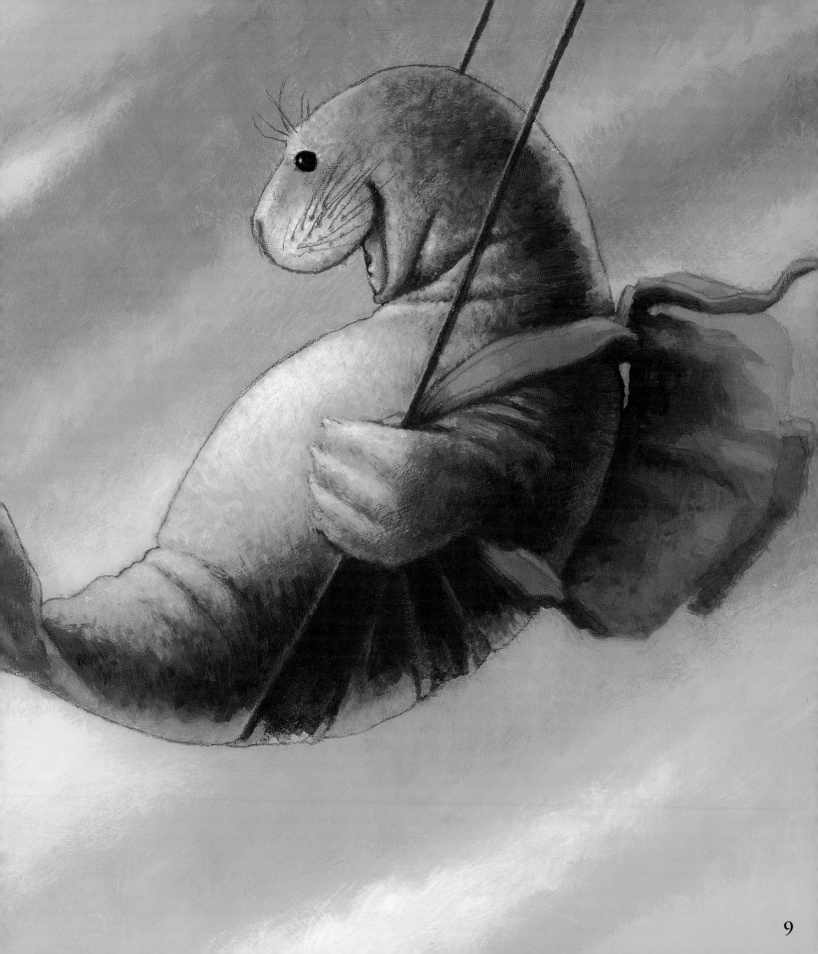

Next morning Koa said,
"I've got a new place to explore,
A town called Hanapēpē.
It's just minutes up the shore."

So off they went, and Koa was right:
This town was the place to be,
With shoreline shops and restaurants
And other things to see.

As the sun was just about to set,
They departed for the day.
Koa headed for the northern skies
And Hilo, for the bay.

As Hilo headed for his home,
He saw a giant sign.
It read, "SPECIAL SEEDS FOR SALE —
AND FOR ONLY A SHORT TIME!"

"What makes them so special?" Hilo asked,
For he really wanted to know,
The owner explained, "From these seeds, my friend,
A kukui tree will grow!"

The kukui tree represents *light*, you see,
And whether it's night or day,
You will never be in darkness
If your *light* shows you the way."

Hilo thought of Koa as his special light,
For Koa had led the way
And found the words to build him up
When he wanted to walk away.

Hilo said, "What a perfect gift
To give to my best friend.
A very special 'Thank you!'
Was the message it would send."

He bought the seeds and opened up
The knapsack on his back.
He carefully placed the seeds inside
Then tightened up each strap.

He took off to the water
And continued on his way,
But discovered something terrible
When he finally reached his bay.

The special seeds were missing!
And upon careful review
He saw a hole in the knapsack
Where they must have fallen through.

He persevered (did not give up!)
He searched both high and low,
But finally called off the search
When there was nowhere else to go.

During a nap, Hilo felt a tap
Just like the day they met.
"There's a party in Hanapēpē," whispered Koa,
"And I hear it's the best one yet!"

When they arrived at the party
It was a wondrous sight,
With limbo lines and dancing vines
At every left and right.

Hilo joined a group of friends
And danced the Hokey-Pokey,
While Koa climbed onto the stage
To do some karaoke.

Just as the music was getting louder
And the dancing was frenzied and faster,
An alarming noise turned everything
Into panic and disaster.

A siren was shrieking
As a warning sign for all —
A hurricane was closing in
And about to make landfall.

The two slapped a high-five
And quickly said goodbye,
Then Hilo headed for the shore
And Koa, for the sky.

When Hilo woke next morning
He went out to walk around,
To see if the hurricane
Had done damage to his town.

The hurricane had changed directions
Since the warning had come forth,
And instead of hitting Hanapēpē town,
It had shifted to the north.

Hilo just stood there looking,
Not knowing what to do,
When a messenger bird showed up and said,
"I have a telegram for you."

Hilo did not want to read it
Afraid of what it would say,
But he took a deep breath and continued,
And he wiped a tear away.

Dear friend, My name is Lele,
And I am Koa's cousin.
The hurricane blasted through our swamp last night
And killed at least a dozen.

I'm afraid your best friend Koa
Did not make it through the night.
Many were just too unprepared
For the hurricane's deadly fight.

I'm sorry that I bring you
Such devastating news.
Anyone who knows Koa knows
He did not deserve to lose.

Hilo crumpled up the note
And threw it on the floor.
"But I was just with Koa," he yelled,
"A few short hours before!"

He cried himself to sleep that night
And hardly slept a wink.
"I've lost my friend forever!"
Was all that he could think.

While moping along the beach one day,
Something slowed his stride.
It was a heavy piece of rope
That was brought up by the tide.

It reminded him of that special day
When they went flying through the air,
And how he found the courage
To overcome his scare.

And then Hilo asked himself,
"If Koa were here today,
Would he want me just lying around
And wasting away the day?"

"A little courage is all I need
When trying something new.
Close my eyes, think happy thoughts,
That's all I have to do!"

Hilo found two driftwood sticks
And made a little cross.
He tied the sticks together
With a heavy piece of moss.

He added shells from the shores
Of Hanapēpē town,
And tightly tied this masterpiece
With the rope that he had found.

On a beach in Hanapēpē
With the masterpiece in hand,
He cleared away a special spot
And placed it in the sand.

Hilo sought new adventures
(even if a little wary),
And thought of Koa every time
He conquered something scary.

Days, and weeks, and months went by,
Until Hilo decided one day,
To go and revisit that special spot
On the shores of Hanapēpē.

When the young monk seal was almost there,
He was taken by surprise,
And as he got right up on it
He could not believe his eyes.

The special cross was still right there,
Just as he'd hoped it would be,
But growing right beside it
...Was a small kukui tree.

31

Additional Highlights

The **kukui tree**, commonly known as the "tree of light," has been the state tree of Hawai'i since 1959. The tree has unique seeds, which contain a large amount of oil, and when lit, can actually be used to provide light.

The **'ō'ō bird** (officially called the "Kaua'i 'ō'ō") is an extinct species. It is believed to have become extinct during the mid 1980s. The exact cause for the bird's extinction is unknown; however most researchers speculate that it was either from a rare rat, a poisonous mosquito, or a devastating hurricane that swept across the island.

Pronunciation Guide

Hanapēpē = [ha-na-pay-pay]
Kaua'i = [kah-oo-ah-ee]
kukui = [koo-koo-ee]
Hilo = [hee-loh]
Lele = [lay-lay]
Koa = [koh-uh]
'ō'ō = [oh-oh]

Mahalo
A Special Thanks

I would like to thank Amanda, Alli, Evann, and Gavin for supporting me through all of the stages of this book and for believing in me during my quest to make my dream become a reality. Thank you to Mom, Dad, Debbie, Jamie, Darla, Jimmy, and Danny for inspiring me throughout my lifetime. Thank you to the Lilly Endowment and the Teacher Creativity Program for making this project possible.

Above all, thank you to God above for watching over me every day of my life.